# Amelia

The boy threw the stone in the air. He swung at it with a small stick, and a loud "crack" echoed across the spring afternoon. He heard his mother call for him to come in for lunch, and took the chance to have one last swing. He let the rock go and another "CRACK" burst out, and was replied with a soft, but audible "thwap." The boy dropped the stick and sprinted inside the house, so as not to miss his favorite meal of pizza rolls and juice.

His last at bat which had created the "thwap," which had been so quick and small that even a mouse could have missed it, changed the course of life for one small bird. The stone had left the stick with quite vigor and had struck a small budding branch in a maple tree. The stone struck a nest of sparrow eggs, and one particularly small blue speckled egg was jostled from its slumber, it rolled out of the nest and fell to the ground below. It then landed on the freshly loosened soil from that of a mole hole and there it sat, alone, except for an army of busy marching ants. They passed it by without even a sideward's glance, eager to harvest the spring's new crops.

Coming home that late afternoon, Mrs. Sparrow found her nest with one less egg and was deeply saddened, but since she lived in a world where nature can sometimes be cruel she accepted the loss and vowed to more closely guard her eggs, as she assumed that some preying falcon or evil rat had stolen the egg out of hunger and desperation. Had she but glanced to the ground directly beneath her, she would have found her egg safe and sound on a pile of loose black earth, but since birds are a bit air headed and because she never even considered looking down, the egg remained unfound. She soon forgot about her missing egg, and continued living as if the whole ordeal never even happened. Soon she was off flitting and flying, preparing for a long spring of feeding

hatchlings, and finding a good bird to

share her nest.

A pale red dawn crept over the bright

afternoon and soon a gentle spring rain

began. It kissed the top of the egg and

soon began to brush the earth away from

beneath it, and so the egg found itself

swirling down a miniscule black and dirty

river. It glided silently past the maple tree

where it began its life, and so left behind

any hopes of being found by its true

mother. As the tiny river picked up speed

it met with the tiny streams from beneath

other trees, and soon the stories from

these trees began to grow as muddied as

the water in which they were carried.  The

trickles grew and twisted, until finally they

had formed a grand 2 inch wide rushing

river that cut a gorge of diminutive

proportions into the new spring dirt.  It

twisted its way past the house of the boy

with the bat, and through a jungle of

grasses where it met a make shift dam

formed from the long and sturdy grasses

from a hard winter and small round

smooth pebbles.  It was at this spot where the egg met the tiny stones and created a small and silent, but perceptible "tap."

These pebbles happened to sit directly outside the home of a mother mouse that was sleeping quietly in her room with her eight newborn mouse babies.  Her petite eggshell ears perked at the invisible clink of the egg against the stones and she awoke with a fearful start.  Because she was a sensible woman she sent her husband out in the warm spring rain to investigate the noise.  He was not gone long when the tip of a tiny egg protruded into her room, followed by a slightly exhausted Mr. Mouse. It was here where the fate of the egg was sealed, beginning with a simple conversation led by Mrs. Mouse. She wanted to keep the egg, and both agreed that it was a good and practical idea, and that they should raise the bird inside, (this was right after deciding that if it did not hatch that a rotten egg would make a lovely and delicate brunch,) because mice, after all, are very sensible creatures. They wrapped the egg in warm soft downy blades of grass

and both Mr. and Mrs. Mouse snuggled up

beside it.

Since mice are sensible, it was only common that they name their children after those who do great things, in hopes that they too, will become great in their own tiny ways.  So, the 8 mice children were named Vincent, Kennedy, Abraham, Franklin, Martin and Luther, Helen, and Pocahontas.  The tiny egg did indeed hatch, and so they named the tiny sparrow Amelia.  They hoped that she too, like her namesake, would become a great flier and sale the world on fantastic adventures, since that is what birds should do.

However, sometimes what we are and who we want to be are two different things. Amelia *WANTED* to be a great flier, with beautiful feathers and grand wings that fanned when she glided over gossamer clouds.

The mice babies knew that Amelia was different and often teased her behind their parent's backs, taunting her about being tossed from the top of a tree before she was even born. (Mice babies are not as sensible or kind as adults.) She heard many comments about her small wings, and yearned for them to grow feathers so that she could spread them and fly away. The sad thing about life is that sometimes it can be a bit cruel. The moment her egg slipped from the nest, Amelia was broken. She lost the necessary warmth that gives young birds the healthy growth they need, and her wings did not form right. They grew in too small, and Amelia, unlike her namesake, would never fly. So, the taunting increased, and Amelia grew older with the knowledge that she would be grounded for life.

It was in the late summer that Mr. and Mrs. Mouse announced that fall was heading their way and that all the 9 children (they now considered Amelia part of their family) should be heading off to start creating their own homes and starting young families of their own. Mice, as a general rule, like to belong to a larger colony when the cold winter months cried out at their door, and Mr. and Mrs. Mouse felt it was time for them to move back to their own colony. The mice children would join the colony once they had found their true loves, and started building their grand families.

Amelia was immediately alarmed, as she had hoped to stay exactly where she was, which was underground and away from taunting eyes and a world of predators. Mr. and Mrs. Mouse had other plans, and pressed her out the door with her 8 brothers and sisters into a world that was neither kind, nor forgiving.  They all

packed up their belongings and made their

way out the door into a warm summer

morning, eager to prove their parents

proud.  Amelia lagged behind with a sullen

slow walk on her little bird feet which were

ill equipped for long journeys by foot.

Birds are meant to fly, not walk, and so

this journey was starting off in a poor way.

As she trudged along through the tall

grasses that were once her home she

began to drag further and further behind

her siblings and soon had absolutely lost

them.

Since it was a warm summer morning, Amelia began to enjoy her brisk walk, even though she wasn't meant to travel by foot.  She had to often pause while she walked, letting her tired feet relax.  Because it was a beautiful day, the walk wasn't as tedious as it could have been, and she was in good spirits.  The warm air encircled her, and on it she could hear birds in the trees around her chirping their hellos, and soon she began to sing along with them.

*Ain't no rain no more no more*

*Summer sun is in the air*

*Hello good morning to the sky*

*We say good night to the moon*

*Lovely day is coming soon*

She started the second verse, and enjoyed the company of those she could not see. Their songs lightened her heart, and soon she was walking briskly down a nice worn path, and quickly forgot the world which was around her. She was focused on the warmth of the morning, the melody that was around her and the fine walk she was on. She was far into the third verse when she realized that the songs of the morning had stopped, and it was only her voice she could hear. She paused, and her tiny sparrow heart began to beat fast. Around her, tall grasses could cover her body, and she had learned to make herself small and still, like mice do, so that she may blend in with that of nature. Instinct told her that there was something near, and the hushed voices of those around her confirmed her suspicions. She could not smell well, and being hidden down so low in tall grasses

gave her no ability to see anything beyond

that which was immediately in front of her.

She drew herself tighter to the ground, and

closed her eyes in hopes that whatever was

out there could not see her. She wished

herself invisible, and almost entirely

stopped breathing. Soon she began to

hear the birds again, and relaxed her body.

The air tasted good in her lungs and she

began to breathe in the warmth. The world

can be a dangerous place for a bird, and it

was doubly dangerous for her. She

scolded herself for singing, knowing that it

could attract a predator.  As she stood up

and stretched, she pledged to be more vigi-

**BAM!**

Something struck her from behind

and she took a flying tumble forward and

landed in a clump of dry summer dirt.

Stunned, she stood up and looked around

to see the large green eyes of a very large

gray cat.

The cat yawned, baring his

enormous fangs to Amelia.  He seemed

sleepy, and bored with her, and she knew

that this was just part of his game.  She

also knew that she had no way of escaping,

and soon the end of her days would be to a

rather large plain gray barn cat.

"Can't you fly?" asked the cat long

and drawn out.

"I can..." whispered Amelia.

"Then fly darling. Escape me so that we may enjoy the chase. I do love a good chase, don't you?" cooed the cat with a fond remembrance in his voice.

"I can fly...." she repeated, knowing that there was uncertainty in her voice. She knew that there was no way to-

The cat pounced before she could finish her thought. Both of his large furry paws pressed her hard into the dry ground. She felt his whiskers brushing against her feathers.  He leaned in and his green eyes danced with excitement.

"I do not think you can fly."

His voice purred with a content malevolence, and he flattened himself down to get a closer look at Amelia.  His eyes grew large and green, and the pupils narrowed.  A large cat smile spread across his eager face.

"I can fly..." this time with a bit more anger in her voice.  Her sensibility from her mouse parents made her a bit annoyed with the cat's repeated question.  "I CAN fly!" she yelled this time, producing a face of anger and frustration.

The cat sat up on his haunches, and blinked his eyes one at a time, with a slow and precise indignity. Amelia wondered if his dinner usually spoke to him with such force, and immediately regretted her tone. Before she had time to apologize for her actions, the cat swiped at her with his paws and knocked her backwards. She sailed a short distance and landed in a mass of feathers with her head face down in the dirt.

"Then fly," ordered the cat, and as he ordered this, he proclaimed that the game was on.

Amelia righted herself and began to hop away, dodging between the drying brush and large gray stones. She fell in between two rocks, and felt the cat's whiskers as he nosed his way in between the crack. He gave a small cat snort and an excited "MEOW" and, Amelia, fearing that this was the end, struck out with her tiny beak and caught the cat's sensitive nose with a quick peck. He yowled and spat, sitting back on his haunches as he patted his tender nose. And Amelia took off once again, hopping as fast as she could go. Her legs hopped to and fro, darting as fast as she could go. Her tiny heart raced with fear, and a new found hope.

"You can not fly, oh what a pity my dear" cooed the cat as he padded behind her with his soft gray feet. He caught up quickly, and batted her once again, sending her tumbling across the ground. Bits of grass and dust clung to her feathers, and she rolled across the dry ground.  Her head was dizzy, and her legs

hurt.  One of her wings was sprained from

the ordeal, and still she continued to hop

even though she was growing tired, and

the cat's batting was causing her to grow

disoriented.  She remembered from stories

that cats often played with their food

before eating it and knew that she had to

do something drastic to escape with her

life.  She looked around, and seeing no

shelter in which to run to, did the last

impractical and brave thing she could do.

She spun around on her heels and hopped

straight for the cat, her head down and was moving as fast as her little legs could go. This move was a good one, and she darted between his legs. The cat was startled as he was not used to his prey running beneath him, he spun a bit too late and tumbled into the dirt. He sat in the dirt, clearly defeated and began to clean himself off. Amelia laughed, despite herself and darted away. She had made it into the woods, and felt a sense of pride and was giddy because of it. She relaxed, and continued her easy stride when something bounded overhead and before her, once again, was the cat. He was crouched low, and as the dark shadow of his body loomed over her, he spoke.

"That was both brave, and foolish," said the cat. "And since you are brave, you shall know my name before you are devoured." The cat sat up proudly, puffed out his chest and declared "My name is Tom."

And with that Tom squatted back on his legs and pounced, covering Amelia with fur and claws, and quickly without word snatched her up in his mouth. The world

went dark for poor Amelia.

Waking up after being

dinner is a very unique experience. Amelia

realized that she should be dead but

instead felt that she was, in fact, very

much alive. In comparison, how she felt to

how she thought she should feel was quite

different. She believed that she should be

sore, bewildered and a bit scared when the reality of the situation was that she was mostly agitated that the cat who called himself Tom had not eaten her. Amelia felt outrage at his inability to eat her. Had she tasted bad? Amelia knew that couldn't be it, and considered herself to taste especially delicious. Was she a later dinner, perhaps? She hoped not, and that he would soon devour her as it had been a long day and she was quite tired.

"Ah darling, so nice of you to wake up."

"Mister Tom..."

"Please dear, call me Tom. Mister sounds sooooo old and stuffy, and saps my energy so," Tom interrupted her, as he purred and rolled slowly on his back with his paws batting the air with a dainty dignity.

"Tom," she started again, gritting her beak down with force, "Would you be grateful enough to just eat me already? I am tired and irritated and would prefer to not go through with that long chase again. I'm very much done with playing around."

"Oh dear," giggled Tom "I couldn't eat YOU. You are a bird and I dare not touch anything that isn't prepared especially for me." And with saying that, he purred, rolled back over onto his feet and arched his back to show Amelia his polished fur.

"I, my dear, am a vegetarian. Most cats aren't, you know. They partake in that nasty habit of eating mice and birds, and other living creatures, but me, I am a spectacular specimen and need to keep myself as such. You see, if I were to chase and eat everything I could, I would lose all interest in keeping myself perfect."

Amelia looked at him clearly confused.

"See my fur? It's so well brushed, not a hair out of place. And my nails are completely manicured. I can't even begin to tell you how much time I spend on my gleaming white teeth. Mice and birds and such would just completely destroy all my hard work, so I watch what and *WHOM* I eat. Its how I keep so magnificent." He brushed his paw over his perfect ears and cleaned his spotless face.

"Ok...now if you had no intention of

eating me...?"

"Oh the charade we played? Darling, I MUST keep up appearances for the neighbors. My vegetarianism would become the laughing stock of everyone here if they were to find out, I mean, a cat that doesn't eat mice and birds!? I simply couldn't let that happen to my self esteem. I'm very fragile you know."  And with that statement, he yawned and stretched with his tail curling in a distinct question mark, and promptly lay down to sleep. His green eyes closed and his whiskers twitched just slightly, as if in fond remembrance of cleanings and preenings.

It wasn't long before Tom was gently snoring, and the adventure of the day began to glaze over in a foggy dream.

Amelia began to relax, as she began to realize that she was in no real apparent danger. Although she was quite sore from the whole ordeal, her body was not injured, aside from the sprain in her wing, and she felt she could stand up and explore her surroundings. She was in some sort of rustic looking building, with wooden walls and golden yellow straw that covered the floor. There was a faint dust in the air, and it glistened in the sunbeams which peaked through the holes and cracks in the wood. It was a beautiful place, and felt warm and inviting. The sun warmed her feathers and she began to plume herself. It wasn't long before the warmth of the sun, and the weight of the day's adventures overpowered her and she soon fell fast asleep.

Amelia woke up and stretched her small aching wings and yawned. The whole ordeal the previous day seemed like a dream, until she glanced around and saw the morning sun peaking in through the dusty cracks in the barn walls. She ruffled her feathers, and fluffed her body out until she was nothing but a large downy ball.

She took the liberty of exploring her temporary home, and soon began to wander in and out of the dry straw that was scattered in piles on the floor. The room smelled wonderful, full of the aroma of long forgotten animals. She hopped from the golden straw onto the dry dirt and peeked her beak out into a new morning, letting the sun tickle her feathers. She fluffed herself again and hopped off in search of a late breakfast.

It wasn't long before she found a small

patch of thistle and began happily pecking away at the tiny seeds from the plants. As she stood there eating a wonderful breakfast she realized that she was not eating breakfast alone. A large dark shadow loomed over her back and her heart sank.

"Good morning my dear Amelia."

She turned to find that Tom had snuck up behind her, and she gave him a long judgmental look for being so sneaky. He, of course, did not notice as he was busy giving himself a thorough cleaning.

Out of boredom and with a full belly she watched him as he carefully went over every detail of his fur, and when he finished he placed his paws by Amelia and stretched his back all the way up to his long luxurious tail. The two remained in good company for some time, sitting and enjoying the beautiful perfection of the morning as it gave way to a beautiful early afternoon. As if they were very old and dear friends, no words needed to be spoken. The pure companionship of the other was all that was required for sometimes the best conversations are one's that desire nothing more than knowing the other person was there.  Amelia was enjoying her new found friend, and happily accepted that this was a place she could stay for a long while.

**"Mr. Tinklebottom!!"**

Both Amelia and Tom flinched at the shout, and Amelia gave a flurried beat of her wings.  Tom instinctively crouched low, his eyes glinting at the sound, which was produced by a young girl in a lovely pink dress.

"Mr. Tinklebottom! You bad kitty!" This time the shout was much lower, and Tom remained crouched by Amelia, he seemed to have lost every bit of dignity at the sound of the shouted words. The girl was walking forward with a very deliberate march, and her hands and arms were swinging with some flustered frustration. As she got closer she began to shoo Tom away, and in between her swats she would occasionally shout things like "bad kitty" and "scat", and "Mr. Tinklebottom." Tom gave Amelia one last sidelong glance, and flattened his ears at the girl and meowed a forlorn apology before bounding off into the tall weeds of a forgotten field.

Amelia's heart was racing as the girl whispered quiet soothing words and slowly reached down to pick her up, all the while murmuring to Amelia in a breathy apologetic voice.

"Awwww poor thing! You are so scared, you are. I scared that nasty cat away. Poor poor thing. Mr. Tinklebottom is an awful cat. Did he hurt you? Bad cat! It's ok little bird, I saved you."

The girl continued her random whispered apologies for some time while carrying Amelia in her cupped hands. The pair trekked over a solid distance before a large white farmhouse emerged ahead of them. As they got closer the doorway loomed ahead of them like the giant black mouth of some hungry creature. It soon swallowed them whole as the girl strode right through it without a moment's hesitation, and Amelia was once again thrust into a panicky darkness.

Once inside the house, Amelia's

eyes began to adjust to the dim light

surrounding her.  She seemed to be in

some sort of large box, and she assumed

that this place was a human house.

There was some sort of large stuffy

rock sitting in the middle of the floor that

the girl stepped around, making sure to

keep Amelia trapped in between her hands. They travelled through another small room, with a lot of light. Amelia was hit with the smells of food and warmth, and immediately liked this room. It felt inviting, and she wouldn't have minded staying there longer, but their trek continued on, up and up until the girl rushed her way into a long narrow room with another door in the middle. The pair made their way through, and the girl spoke again.

"Chipper has a new friend," cooed the

girl, and she struggled with some large wire box which she placed Amelia into.

Above her, perched on a round stick was a green and blue bird with the most gorgeous colors Amelia had ever seen. His long tail swung down to where Amelia was placed on the floor of the cage, and as she looked up she met with his curious black eyes.

"Pretty bird!" He cackled at the new guest in his cage.

Amelia blushed and curtsied at his compliment.

"Pretty bird!" He repeated with the same candor.

"Thank you..." Amelia whispered.

"Pretty bird!" And with that he turned and climbed into the small bird house that hung in his cage.

"How strange," thought Amelia.

She looked around the wire cage and began a short uneventful exploration of her current surroundings. She looked over the edge and found that her room was up in the air, hanging on some sort of shiny stick. It was roughly fifty hops around,

and she was able to climb up to the top
which she felt was rather high for a bird of
her disposition. She climbed down to
where the beautiful blue green bird had sat
and noticed a sort of polished stone that
stood as tall as her. She scrambled over to
it and was astounded to see another bird
staring back at her.

"Hello."

Nothing.

**"Hello!"**

More nothing.

**"HELLO!"**

Silence, although the bird was hopping back and forth much like Amelia herself. She felt that she was being teased, and so decided to give the bird a quick peck to show him that she was less than impressed. As she moved her beak forward, so did the bird and as her beak collided with the polished stone she realized that there was no other bird there.

She stumbled back in slight astonishment, and then moved up close to inspect the other bird. As she stood irritated and staring at the bird stuck in a stone she noticed that it had wings like hers.

"You're like me!" Amelia laughed. She'd never met another bird like herself, and if this one was like her, then maybe this was the perfect place for her to live! Maybe, over in the stone that bird was happy! She gave her wings a flap and a rustle and watched as the other bird did exactly the same. She moved up close and peered with one eye at it, and the other bird moved up with her. Every move she made the other bird repeated in exactly detail right along with her. They moved in tandem, and Amelia was growing frustrated.

"Pretty bird!" blasted a large squawk from behind her, and the beautiful bird pushed Amelia out of the way to get to the polished stone. He passed her a glaring, jealous look before he peered into the polished stone, and Amelia saw that another bird exactly like him was peering back. It was at that precise moment that she realized that there was no other bird, but just a trick of the polished stone.

Amelia sadly climbed back down the side of the wired box and hid beneath rustling papers and cried herself to sleep.

The late night chatter of mice woke Amelia up.  She heard them whispering in the walls, and beneath the floor.  Although she couldn't quite understand their muffled words, she knew something big was happening.  Mice talk incredibly fast when they are excited and because she grew up in a mouse household, Amelia recognized the squeaking for what it was, panic and fear.

The shrill mouse voices continued throughout the night, and Amelia drifted in and out of sleep. Her mind was plagued by dreams of large gray cats, wire houses that held her wings down and a blue sky that she would never fly in.

The morning broke and Amelia awoke to find that she was being stared at by two huge blue eyes.

"Good morning Mrs. Chatter!"

Amelia stared blankly at the girl who had begun to slowly open the bird cage.

"Mr. Chatter needed a wife, and since that nasty cat was trying to eat you...now

YOU can be his wife!"

Amelia could not understand this, of course, as birds can't speak human. But the excited ranting was clear enough for her to grasp. This child intended to keep her here, with this crazy bird that spoke to himself. Now Amelia was looking to find a home of her own, but spending the rest of her life caged up until she was just as crazy as Mr. Chatter was not her idea of home. Birds are not meant to be caged, for they were given wings for a reason and Chatter's antics proved that a lifetime of a skyless prison could do the worst sort of things to a bird and Amelia was not anxious to experience this first hand.

As she was lost in thought on how to escape a large child's hand had crept into the cage. It was hovering above her when Amelia snapped to attention and began shrilly fluttering as best as her tiny useless wings could go. Her heart began humming in fear, and she began to panic and peck at the hand. She landed one or two solid strikes and the hand retreated, but not before returning to fill the seed and water supply.  The eyes peered in again, and watched her for some time.  The girl wondering if Mrs. Chatter, aka Amelia, would eat or lay an egg and then growing bored of the cowering bird left with nothing more than a quick backwards glance at the birds in the cage.

The day was dull and uneventful, other than the morning routine, and Amelia began to understand why the other bird would talk to himself.  Several times she tried to have a real conversation with him, but "Pretty bird" was all he could muster, and usually was speaking to himself while staring longingly into the mirror.

With nothing better to do, Amelia hopped over to the seed container and picked through the various nuts and seeds. Every once in awhile she found a dried berry and ate with some voracity.

Night came slowly, and that night, she again heard the commotion of the mice and wondered what could be going on. It continued until she fell asleep and had a dreamless night.

The next day was more of the same. The girl would appear, try to grab Amelia and then leave new seeds and change the water. That night was more mouse commotion and Amelia would wake and repeat the days.

This continued for some time, and with the days blending and the nights filled with the excited and labored shouts of mice, Amelia soon forgot how long she was actually in the cage. To fill the voids of the days she began to eat. It wasn't long before Amelia grew plumper and plumper.

Her downy feathers soon poofed out on their own and she was quite a round ball of fluff. She would wobble around the cage, and took to napping for short spurts during the day when her time was not spent eating. Her exasperated attempts to escape the hand became less and less, and soon the girl was able to pick Amelia up with no hesitation.

The girl was gentle, and would cup her hands around Amelia. It was warm and inviting, and soon she would fall asleep in the dark hands that held her. It was times such as these that the cage didn't seem as awful as it once had, and a strange familiar comfort began to surround Amelia. During the mornings, she would wait for the hands, and during the day she would stuff herself with seeds and dried fruit, and the evenings would come and bring the dreams.

At first these dreams were of the outdoors and fresh air. Soon, they became of Amelia struggling to sing, her voice would be torn away by the wind and rain. They grew increasingly sad and when the mornings would come, she would long for the warmth of the hands so that she could fall asleep with no dreams to haunt her.

There were nights where the mice were so loud that Amelia wasn't able to fall asleep at all, and it was these nights where she felt the most normal. She never ate at night, but would sit with her head tilted to the side listening and trying to decipher the words behind the walls.

It had been months since Amelia

was captured and placed in her caged

home.  She had stopped trying to escape,

and freely allowed the girl to handle her

whenever she wanted.  Days were dull, and

the nights brought her vivid dreams or the

agitated mice.

It was during one of those particularly

fitful dreams that the most unusual thing happened.

"Psssssssst"

"Pssssssst"

**"PSSSSSSST"**

It was the final "pssst" that woke Amelia up. She sleepily opened her eyes to find that she was staring at a very large brown mouse. He was unlike the mice she knew from her mother and father, as he was much larger, and while they had delicate seashell like ears, his were scarred and thick. His fur was much darker too, with splashes here and there of soot and dust. His whiskers stuck out like long straws from his face, and he wiggled them inquisitively at Amelia, waiting for her to answer back to him. His eagerness exhausted Amelia, and she shooed him away and turned to go back to her restless sleep.

"I have come on behalf of the mice."

It was all he said, and he again waited for a reaction from her. Since he seemed to be waiting, and would continue to wait, she decided to just hear him out so that he would leave her alone and she could continue on with her life and her slumber.

"Yes?" she answered a bit annoyed.

"We need your help."

At this, Amelia woke up. No one had ever asked for HER help. She was always the one asking for help.

"I'm sorry?"

"We, the mice, have come to ask for your help."

"I'm not sure you need or want my help."

The mouse sighed at this, and wiggled

his long whiskers at her and leaned in further.

"We are aware that you are stuck in this cage, and we can arrange a prison break for you, but in return we need your help."

"I'm quite content here" stated Amelia quite firmly. She turned her back and intended to go back to sleep when the mouse spoke once more.

"Don't you dream of flying again?"

It was those words that sparked Amelia's heart, and she became teary eyed as she answered in a gaspy whisper.

"More than anything."

"We can help. We just need some help in return."

"Go on" she urged, with her head tilted toward the mouse, and her eye studying him intently.

"Let me start with a story."

The mouse cleared his throat, and continued.

"We've lived here in the house, peacefully for 150 mouse generations. We've accepted the cat, Tom, and the others that move in and out. We've shared our home with snakes, other mice, humans and anyone else that moves in."

He paused, allowing Amelia to understand how generous and open they were as creatures.

"Recently, however, our home has been under attack from a new group of mice that have moved in. We've been at war, pushing against their tyranny. They steal our food, and our children grow hungry. We are losing this war, and we are afraid of what will happen to those around us once we have been forced from our homes.  Winter is almost upon us, and all of us, all of our families, will surely freeze and die without the warmth of our homes."

He once again paused, curiously gauging Amelia's response.

"Once again I'm asking you for your help."

Amelia paused, took a deep breath, and said "What do you need me to do?"

It was a cold dark fall night when

Amelia awoke.  The moon shone down

through cracks in the floorboards of the

porch.  She could see the tiny clouds of

breath from the mice that surrounded her.

She looked up into the sky and watched

the slim fingernail of the crescent moon

waning in the deep black sky.  Tiny stars

sparkled like slivers of ice, and it was at that moment that Amelia wished more than anything that she could fly. She cried tears that did not flow, and stared at the sky and cursed it for giving her wings that did not work.

The only world she knew was one that had been giftless and every day that she could not lift herself up to the sky she felt more broken.

As Amelia sat there in her own thoughts, the mice around her began to wake. Brutus sat up beside her, and his eyes gleamed in the broken moon light that fell upon them.

"It's time" was all he whispered.

Amelia nodded and stood up. Her legs felt weak and her mind ached from the decision she was taking part in.

The mice had promised her new wings. They said that they collected trinkets, and bits of things, and could craft her working wings, not made of feather, but of leather and metal. They would be better than her wings, and she could finally touch the sky she so longed for.

They only asked a small, tiny, insignificant favor in return. It was nothing really, and all she had to do was follow their instructions. It was a decision that she made quickly, eagerly, and with a hopeful desire.

Her task was easy enough, and yet she felt a pit in the bottom of her stomach. It was requested that she scare off the advancing mice, so that these mice could once again flourish in the house.

She set off quickly, and quietly, with the package tucked under her tiny wing.

She had to only sprinkle the dust on the food of the new mice. Brutus told her that it was a powder that would give them a belly ache, and they'd hate the food and would leave. If she could corrupt their food, and just push them away, then everyone could be happy once again.

Amelia was nervous that someone would get really sick, but Brutus assured her that no one would suffer, and that even Caesar himself couldn't have been safer in the hands of his loyal following.

She was now winding through the

path beneath the house, listening to the rattling leaves that shook in the trees outside the house. They sounded like the very bones of the dead, around her, urging her to both continue forward and to leave and never come back. Her feet pushed her towards the goal, which meant wings for her and a home for the mice and it was this thought that she focused on.

Ahead of her, in the low light, was a stock pile of food. Amelia took a deep breath, and crept up beside it. In the darkness, she saw very little but knew that she was carefully shaking the contents of the pouch onto the food.

It was quick work, a mere couple of seconds, and then she stepped back and deep remorse filled inside of her. Her head hung low, and slowly she turned around, and began to make her way back to the mice.

She had taken a few footsteps

when she heard voices approaching from

behind her.  Her first thought was that she

was caught, and her heart froze in fear.

She quickly realized that they were

stopping by the food pile, and her curiosity

was unwavering as it forced her to turn

around to see what would happen.

The mice could not see her, and all

she could see of them was a roughly dark

outline. They approached the food, and

snuck a few nibbles of food off. Amelia

expected them to get horrible belly aches,

and cry out over their food. She

anticipated having to run back to the mice

and let them know that it was done. She

imagined that they mice that were sick

would know that she had done it, and her

guilt forced a million other scenarios in her

head. She did foresee all of this in her

head, but she did not prepare for the

actuality of what did happen. Both mice in front of her dropped without words. There were no accusations thrown out about the food, and neither of the mice appeared to have noticed that the food had been tampered with. One second they were eating, and the next they were on the ground in two small dark lumps.

It was in this instant that Amelia had two choices laid out before her; run to the mice that had fallen, or run to the mice that had caused it.

She chose the former.

Her dark path was set before her, and she followed it. She darted to the mice which had fallen, and found them not breathing. She shook them vigorously, hoping that they had simply fallen asleep. No amount of shaking could wake the mice, and Amelia's heart set to panic mode. She began frantically looking around for more mice, for someone,

anyone that she could scream to that she

was sorry, that it wasn't her fault, that

they were just sick. She beat her wings in

a frantic attempt to fly away, but they were

still useless, and no amount of flapping

would cause them to be anything but

broken.

She began to run down the corridor,

towards the home of the mice, hoping to

warn someone before more mice ate the

food which she had deliberately poisoned.

It seemed quiet, and as she ran she

yearned for the mice to be gone. Her guilt was growing inside her, and it was forming a fear deep in the pit of her stomach. What would she say? How would she tell the mice that she had poisoned two of their friends? What would the mice say to her?

These questions began to gently eat at Amelia, tugging at her conscience, and again, she was given a choice: lie or truth. A lie could still accomplish what she needed, saying that she had found the two mice and when she realized what happened she had wanted to warn the mice. No one would know, and everyone would still be safe. No one would judge her for poisoning their friends, and everyone would be happy that Amelia had come to the rescue of those around her. She could go on with life and the mice could go on with theirs.

Maybe she could even tell the OTHER mice that she had tried, and had been caught and had to plan a daring escape. She could still get her wings, and could still warn the mice of the food. Everyone would win, and no one would be the wiser.

She could leave this not only a hero, but a rewarded hero.

She was lost in her thoughts, and the idea of being a hero for the mice when she rounded a corner and ran straight into her own mother mouse.

There, before her, stood the

truth. In all its simplicity, and all the

shame that would come with it. No one

would know the truth, unless she, Amelia

told it. It was horrid, and ugly, and made

her out to be stupid and wrong, but it was

the truth and if she lied and walked away a

hero, it would be a lie and she wouldn't BE

a hero, she would be a lie and it would be

with her for the rest of her life.

Amelia broke down into tears,

recounting the events that lead up to her

poisoning the mice's food. Her mother

looked at her with silent eyes, watching

and waiting for the end of the story.

Amelia told of the cat, and the woods, and

the bird and the girl, and of the mice. She

told every detail of everything, and left

nothing out. When she finished, she wiped her eyes with her broken wings and realized that through all of this, that her own desire to fly to be unbroken is what caused the unnecessary death of two wonderful mice. Her own sense of self loathing had created a dark monster within her, and yet she finished the story. She told her mother up to the end, and when it was over, her mother said nothing and did nothing but sit there.

Mice are very practical creatures, so when something so impractical is presented before them, it takes them a moment to create a practical approach to fixing the impractical problem.

Amelia stood before the mouse that had taken in her egg, had raised her like family, and had provided her with love and food and a home. She stood before the mouse that was the only family she had truly known. Amelia stared at her mother, and without realizing that she was doing it, she began to walk away. She began to walk from the fear of almost killing her family, the fear of betraying those whom she had trusted and loved, and the fear that she almost became more monster than bird. And as her mother watched her, unspeaking, Amelia walked out of their lives forever.

Mother mouse merely nodded to Amelia, knowing that she would never see her again. She did not cry out for her to come back, did not cry out at all in fact, for she had to take care of business. She had to warn the mice of the food situation, and let the colony know what happened. She may leave out a few details, just the unimportant ones, for as practical as Mrs. Mouse is, she was also a loving and caring mouse.

The rats, for that is what they were, not mice, but rats, because only rats would be capable of so many lies; lies to Amelia about wings that work, lies to Amelia about them being mice, in fact, and for poisoning the food supply of the mouse colony. Only rats are selfish enough to want an entire house to for theirselves, and only rats would be cowardly enough to make other's do what they cannot. The rats were taken care of in a practical and careful way, and were never heard or seen from again.

The mice replenished their own food supply, since the old food supply had mysteriously disappeared somewhere behind the house and near a certain undisclosed porch.

Amelia had begun walking, and

had left the house in a fog of her own

mind.

It was fall, and the days had not yet begun

to grow cold, but the nights would create a

delicate and peaceful mist which began to

freeze in the early mornings, before the

sun could kiss the sky with its pink and

gold lips.

Amelia continued to walk, through the cold nights and warm days. Around her leaves changed from green to yellow to brown and fell at her feet. Each decaying leaf reminded her of the broken wings on her back, and they lay as lifeless as the leaves on the ground.

She walked over ground which began to harden and close itself up for the upcoming winter.

Plants shriveled, leaves fell, and the world began to change. Winter winds began to hug the trees, slowly at first. The cold was so secret and quiet that it was almost unnoticed. Then, it grew until it brought the first snow of the season, which sifted a fine white powder onto the cold and frozen earth.

The winter winds tore across the world, spreading more and more snow, and soon the world changed again, from early winter to deep winter and snow covered everything in a blanket of glittering white. Animals hid away, waiting out the harsh cold days until spring would come and wake them with the gentle caress of the sun and the soft warm breath of spring winds.

Through all of this Amelia walked. Through the snow and cold, she walked. And as the world began to change, so did Amelia. She had left the house that night with a fluffy feathery coat, and bright shiny eyes, and a wonderful happy song.

As she walked, she began to lose the shine to her eyes, and she refused to sing and she refused to eat or sleep. Feathers began to fall off, as she stopped preening and cleaning the feathers she had. Her body grew thin, and as the winter months pressed on, Amelia walked. If an animal happened to poke its head out for a breath of fresh air it would see a small walking bird skeleton, driven by the sadness of what she had become. She did not consider herself a bird, nor did she consider herself a mouse. She was a flightless form that would walk until she was eaten, or until she simply ceased to live.

Animals avoided her, making wide

paths around the ghost that walked

through the snow.

And the winter poured around her,

snow pushed against her, and the world

was angry for her.

And Amelia walked.

Through the snow, and the wind.

And Amelia walked.

The winter months dragged on.

And Amelia walked.

And the winter months grew less wintery.

And Amelia walked.

And the winter months began to pass, and spring soon began to show itself again. And the world grew hopeful, and the sun began to warm the ground, and from it sprang tiny shoots of green grass. And the warmth of the spring air awakened those which had slumbered through the winter. They yawned and stretched and ventured out into the world once again.

And through it all, Amelia had walked, until she had nothing more than  sticks for feathers, and the cold had bitten her legs and feet, leaving her scarred and broken. Her wings were nothing more than tiny black stumps upon her back, and her body was nothing more than a whisper of a bird. And still death had not taken her, for she was the walking dead.  Her misery dragged her through this world, half alive, unwanted by even the hungriest of cat and fox.  And as the sun touched her with its warmth, she could not feel it, for the

coldness in her heart ran so deep that it

could not be warmed by the touch of

golden rays of spring's sun.

All around her new life was springing

forth, and yet all she saw was her own

guilt, her own deceit.

She walked slower now, but still

walked. She knew that time was coming to

a close for her, and that she would die in

the first hours of some spring morning, but

she continued to walk.

Sparrows in love swooned around her,

dipping and diving, singing songs of love and freedom. Wild flowers had begun to peek through the fresh warm dark earth that she walked through, tiny green fingers pressing through and grasping at a blue sky. Amelia saw none of this.

And as she slowed down, her head grew heavy and her sight grew dim, and in front of her eyes that did not see were earthworms that wriggled free to watch her.

It was then, in the last moments of her existence that a song pierced the

shards of ice which surrounded her heart.
At first it was a soft and luxurious song,
like the warm cashmere fur of a young
kitten. Then the song began to grow,
proud, warm and beautiful, like the song of
the wind. And it smoothed out, and grew
dark and sad, and finally finished as a
silky and smooth as the water over rocks.

Amelia found some small amount of
energy and began to crawl to the source of
the song, it was bother her curiosity and
the power of the song which moved her.
There were no words, but it was a song of

the heart. And as Amelia crawled her way to the source she began to see her life in his song. She saw strength, and family, and she saw Tom the cat, with his loving green eyes and his beautiful gray fur, and she the girl which had taken her in, who had the warm comforting hands that surrounded her when she needed it. She saw the nest she was born in, and she saw the mice taking in an egg which should never have hatched. She saw her wings, broken and lifeless. And she saw herself poisoning those that had cared for her when no one else in the world would. She saw herself walking month after month in a cold cruel world, one that was neither as cold nor cruel as she had first imagined.

She crawled to the tree which housed the bird that sang. And as he sang, his words touched the world, and animals stopped frolicking in the warmth of the sun, and insects no longer buzzed, and even the clouds themselves paused to hear the song of the bird in the tree. He sang deep and pure, an opera of life which called for everyone to turn their ears and imagine their own lives.  And as Amelia

leaned against the tree her sorrow was

lifted.  It was in this song, and her

happiness that Amelia's world went dark

for the last time.

Amelia awoke sore, tired, and

hungry. Before her sat an elegant blue jay,

who seemed to radiate with the rays of the

sun. His wing was cradling Amelia, with a

gentle and loving caress. He lifted her

head, and Amelia found that he was gently

feeding her fresh thistle seeds. She ate,

which hurt, and she coughed and

somewhere within her, a smile formed.

He did not speak, but urged her to eat some more, which she did with a tender quiet sort of way. It pained her to eat, and with every piece she would grimace, but he continued feeding her unwavering in his attempt.

All the while, she watched him with wonder. Was this the bird that was singing? Why did he sing without words? What was his song about? Although she knew the answer to this, for he sang about life, love, the sun, darkness and cold and betrayal.  His song was everything and nothing rolled into one.  It was pure power, and horrible weakness.  He spoke not a word, but simply urged Amelia to eat and to live.

She did not know why he wanted her to live, but she ate and felt a bit of strength returning to her feeble and broken body. She wanted to scream out that his was a lost cause, that her life was worth nothing, but she knew that he would ignore this and continue trying.  So, instead of crying out, she ate and watched and waited to speak.

"who are you?" her hoarse and tired voice whispered, almost too quiet to hear after months of walking in a dark silence.

He spoke no word to her, but continued feeding her.

And as he reached for the piles of seeds, Amelia realized that he was blind. His gossamer wings, and beautiful feathers gleamed, and he saw none of this. He did not see Amelia's withered and bony body. He did not see the black stumps where her broken wings ceased to exist. He saw nothing, but he knew she was there. He knew that she was in need, and provided it. He asked for nothing, but gave what he could.

As Amelia lay there, held by the gentle power of his wing, she knew why: because he was broken, because he was without a family, because he was more than a bird without sight. And it was then that Amelia understood everything.

And as she looked up into his kind face, she knew love too. And she knew that he saved her because he loved her.

He loved her like he loved the sky, and the earth, and the world around her. And Amelia knew that life was more than wings and flying, that life was what she had made it, and that her wings were not what defined her, but only a part of her. Her world was what she wanted it to be, and it could be as powerful and wonderful as she decided.

And inside her was a rolling sea of new hope and of dreams that could come true. Inside of his silent warm embrace the world became everything Amelia had ever dared dream it could be.

And as she looked into his sightless

eyes Amelia knew she was home.

Jessica was born in Michigan, and after several years in college at Grand Valley, and several years teaching she moved to Indiana. She now lives there happily with her fiancé and their 2 dogs.